Other titles available:

Blue Saves the Day

Doug the Busy Digger

Fairy Sunshine

Rags the Brave Puppy

The Troublesome Twins

ISBN 1-84135-235-7 (cased)
ISBN 1-84135-252-7 (limp)

First published 2003

Published by Award Publications Limited,
27 Longford Street, London NW1 3DZ

Printed in Malaysia

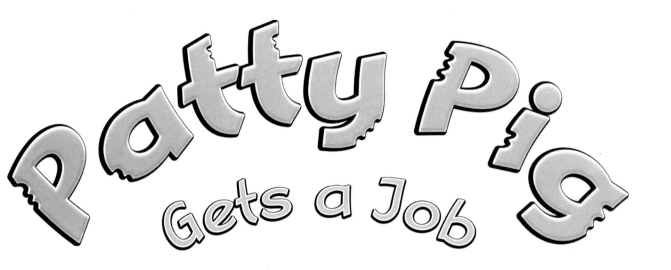

Patty Pig
Gets a Job

Written by Lesley Rees
Illustrated by Gary Rees

AWARD PUBLICATIONS LIMITED

Every animal on Sunnyside Farm has an important job to do.

MOO-MOO! MOO-MOO! The cows supply tasty, creamy milk for the farmer's children to drink.

CLIP-CLOP! CLIP-CLOP!

The horse pulls the cart that takes
the farmer's wife to market.

CLUCK-CLUCK! CLUCK-CLUCK!
The hens lay lots of speckled
eggs for the family's breakfast.

BAA-BAA! BAA-BAA! The cuddly sheep give up their fleeces to make soft, warm wool, which the farmer's wife knits into nice warm jumpers.

BAA-BAA! BAA-BAA!

All the animals are kept very busy. All except one – Patty Pig.

All day long, Patty lies in her sty, wallowing, eating and snoozing. She doesn't see why she should do anything to help around the farm and doesn't care what the other animals think.

"My job is wallowing, eating and snoozing,"
she grunts. "And I'm very good at it."

But the other animals aren't happy. It really isn't fair. Patty has such an easy life.

"Let's find her a job!" neighs Henry Horse.

And all the other animals agree.

"But I've got a job," snorts Patty.
"Wallowing, eating and snoozing!"

PIGS DON'T WORK!

The animals take no notice. "Come on!" they cry.
"Let's find you something useful to do."

"Okay, okay," she oinks.
"I'm coming. But I CAN'T
give milk...

... and I DON'T
lay eggs!

So what CAN I do?"

"You can pull my cart," says Henry, popping the harness over Patty's head. "Come on, off you trot."

But it isn't very long before it all goes wrong. WIBBLE-WOBBLE-WIBBLE-

BANG!

Poor Patty can't trot fast enough and the cart keeps banging her big pink bottom.

"OWWW!" she cries. "Please give me something else to try."

QUACK!

"I know," miaows Chivers Cat, "you can help me catch mice in the barn."

But those naughty, scampering mice just run round and round, until Patty is so dizzy, she collapses in a heap!

"Never mind," woofs Shep Sheepdog.
"Come and help me round up the sheep."
"Okay," grumbles Patty, "but I don't
think I'll be any good at it."

And she's right. When she trots into the field, the sheep stand very, very still and just laugh and laugh. Patty feels very silly!

"See!" she snorts, grumpily. "I told you. There's nothing I can do! I'm going back to my sty for a snack and a snooze. I don't want to be disturbed."

So Patty waddles back through the farmyard towards her sty, completely unaware that she's being followed.

All the baby animals on the farm are flapping, trotting, wobbling and waddling behind Patty.

The little animals see how warm and cuddly Patty looks, and think she's just right to snuggle up to!

Patty settles in the straw for a nap.
Quickly, the babies flap, trot and wobble
into her sty and snuggle against her.

Patty is very surprised, but she doesn't mind and gives them all a big cuddle. In no time at all, everyone is fast asleep and snoring – ZZZzzzz.

When the mummies and daddies stop work for the day, they can't believe their eyes. Patty has found the perfect job after all. She's the farm's very own babysitter!

Now, when all the animals are working, Patty is working too, looking after all the babies on Sunnyside Farm.

To Robin and Eunice *R L S*

For Jack and Edna *T K*

First published in Great Britain in 2004
by Orion Children's Books
a division of the Orion Publishing Group Ltd
Orion House
5 Upper St Martin's Lane
London WC2H 9EA

Text © Ruth Louise Symes 2004
Illustrations © Tony Kenyon 2004

Design by Tracey Cunnell

A catalogue record for this book is available from the British Library.

Printed in Italy

ISBN 1 84255 264 3

Floppy Ears

Story by **Ruth Louise Symes**

Illustrations by **Tony Kenyon**

Orion
Children's Books

One day Twitchy Nose said, 'Can I go and play with my friends?'
'Can I go too?' said Floppy Ears.
'You're too little!' said Twitchy Nose.
'Take Floppy Ears with you or you don't go,'
said Mum. 'And make sure the fox doesn't see you.'
'Oh all right, come on then, Floppy Ears,' said
Twitchy Nose. 'You'll have to run fast
to keep up with me.'

'Hello,' said Twitchy Nose's friends,
Sneezer and Bendy Whiskers.

'Mum said I had to bring Floppy Ears with me,'
said Twitchy Nose. 'What shall we play? I know,
let's play hopping. I'm very good at hopping.'

'Can I play?' said Floppy Ears.
'No – you're too little to hop properly,'
said Twitchy Nose.

'So what can I do?' said Floppy Ears.
'You can watch,' said Twitchy Nose.

So Floppy Ears sat under the big old oak tree and watched Twitchy Nose and Sneezer and Bendy Whiskers hopping.

Floppy Ears thought Twitchy Nose was very good at hopping.

'Let's play racing now. I'm very good at racing,'
said Twitchy Nose.

'Can I play?' said Floppy Ears.
'No – you're too little to race properly.'

'So what can I do?'
'You can watch.'

So Floppy Ears sat under the
old oak tree and watched
Twitchy Nose and Sneezer
and Bendy Whiskers racing.

Floppy Ears thought Twitchy Nose was very good at racing.

'Let's play jumping over sticks now. I'm very good at jumping over sticks,' said Twitchy Nose.

'Can I play?' said Floppy Ears.
'No – you're too little to jump properly.'

'So what can I do?'
'You can watch.'

So Floppy Ears sat under
the old oak tree and watched
Twitchy Nose and Sneezer
and Bendy Whiskers playing
jumping over sticks.

Floppy Ears thought Twitchy Nose was very good at jumping.

'We have to go home now,' said Sneezer and Bendy Whiskers. 'That's OK,' said Twitchy Nose. 'I wanted to play by myself anyway. I'm going to play being a Mummy Rabbit.'

'Can I play?' said Floppy Ears.
'No — you're too little to play being
a Mummy Rabbit.'

'So what can I do?' said Floppy Ears.

But Twitchy Nose was too busy playing to answer.
'I know what I can do,' Floppy Ears said. 'I can watch.'

While Floppy Ears was watching, the fox came over the hill.

'Twitchy Nose! Twitchy Nose!
The fox is coming!' cried Floppy Ears.

But it was too late.
The fox had seen them.

Floppy Ears and Twitchy Nose ran away as fast as they could.

'Quick! Let's hide in here,' said Floppy Ears.
Twitchy Nose and Floppy Ears jumped into
a blackberry bush and kept very still.

The fox looked one way

and then it looked the other.

But it couldn't see Floppy Ears and Twitchy Nose.
They stayed quite, quite still until the fox had gone.

'Did you let Floppy Ears play?' Mum asked,
when Twitchy Nose and Floppy Ears got safely home.
'Oh yes,' said Floppy Ears. 'We played hide and seek.
We're very good at hiding.'
        And Twitchy Nose said, 'Please can Floppy Ears
come out to play again tomorrow?'

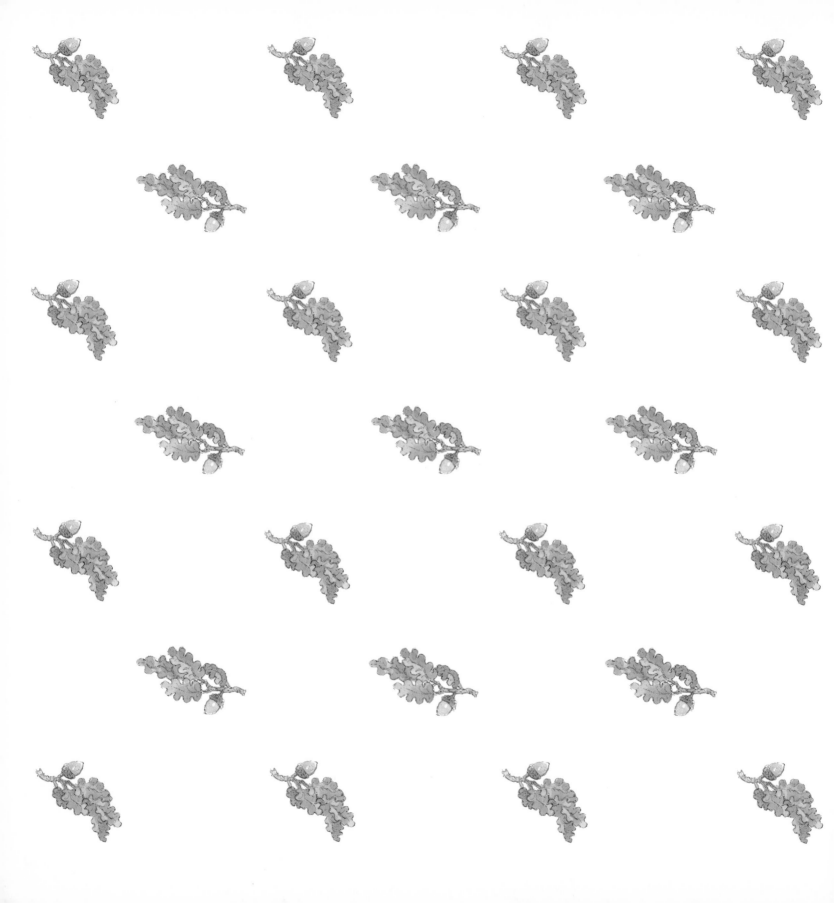